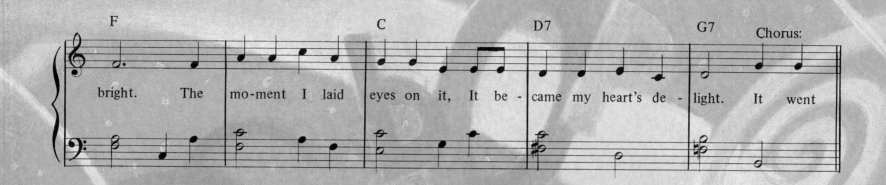

bright. The mo-ment I laid eyes on it, It be - came my heart's de - light. It went

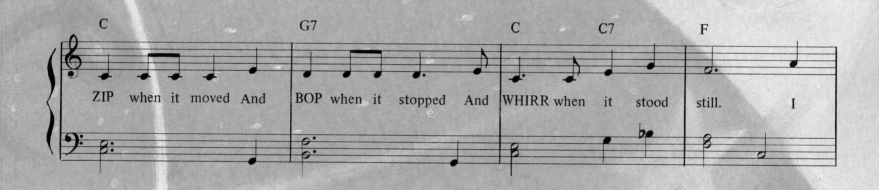

ZIP when it moved And BOP when it stopped And WHIRR when it stood still. I

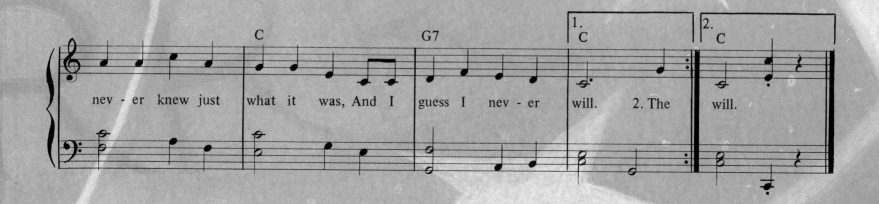

nev - er knew just what it was, And I guess I nev - er will. 2. The will.

TOM PAXTON

the MARVELOUS TOY

illustrated by Elizabeth Sayles

MORROW JUNIOR BOOKS ☆ New York

Pastels were used for the full-color illustrations.
The text type is 17-point Bookman.

Text copyright © 1996 by Tom Paxton
Music and words copyright © 1961, 1989 by Cherry Lane Music Publishing Company, Inc.
Illustrations copyright © 1996 by Elizabeth Sayles

Printed in the United States of America.

1 2 3 4 5 6 7 8 9 10

Library of Congress Cataloging-in-Publication Data
Paxton, Tom.
The marvelous toy/by Tom Paxton; illustrated by Elizabeth Sayles.
p. cm.
Summary: A father gives to his young son the same marvelous toy
that his father had given to him many years before.
ISBN 0-688-13879-9 (trade)—ISBN 0-688-13880-2 (library)
[1. Toys—Fiction.   2. Fathers and sons—Fiction.   3. Stories in rhyme.]
I. Sayles, Elizabeth, ill.   II. Title.   PZ8.3.P2738Mar 1996
[E]—dc20   95-35384   CIP AC

To Kate, who is all grown up now,
but who is still a Rare Gem
—T.P.

To my parents, for the toys they gave us,
and to Ma, for the ones she saved
—E.S.

When I was just a wee little lad
Full of health and joy,
My father homeward came one night
And gave to me a toy.

A wonder to behold it was
With many colors bright.
The moment I laid eyes on it,
It became my heart's delight.

It went **ZIP** when it moved
And **BOP** when it stopped
And **WHIRR** when it stood still.
I never knew just what it was,
And I guess I never will.

The first time that I picked it up
I had a big surprise,
For right on the bottom were two big buttons
That looked like big green eyes.

I first pushed one and then the other,
Then I twisted its lid.
And when I set it down again,
This is what it did:

It went **ZIP** when it moved
And **BOP** when it stopped
And **WHIRR** when it stood still.
I never knew just what it was,
And I guess I never will.

It first marched left and then marched right,
Then marched under a chair.
And when I looked where it had gone,
It wasn't even there!

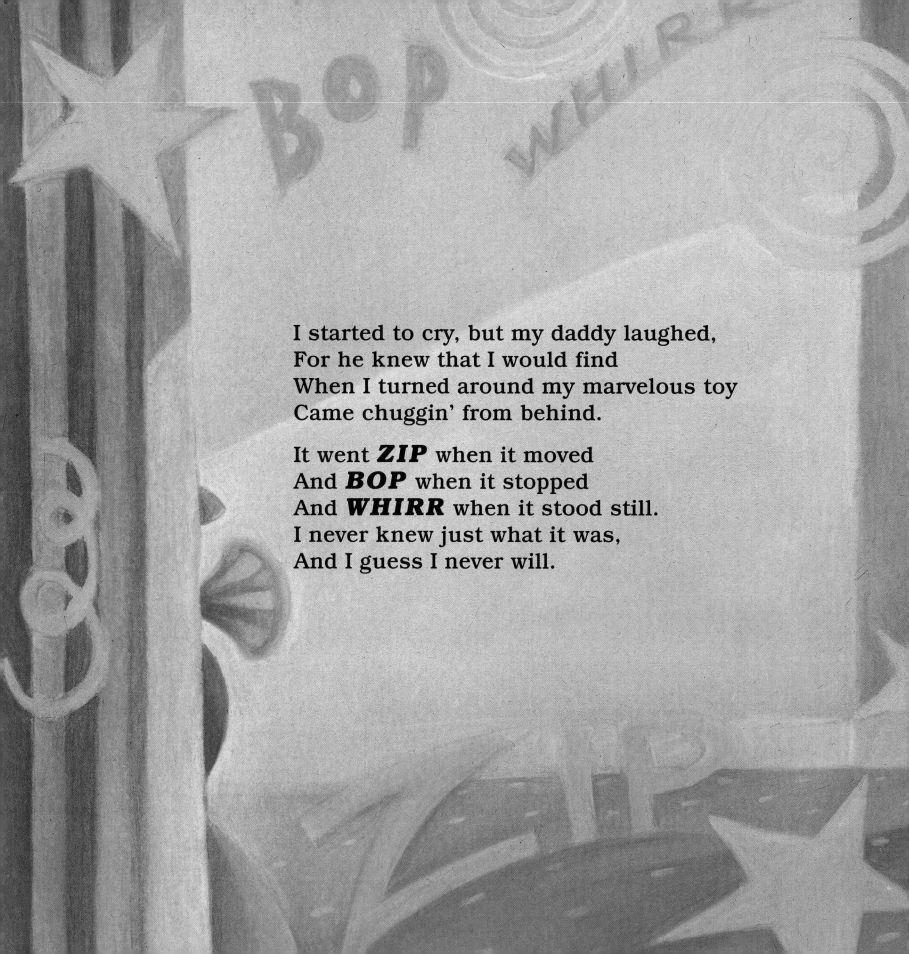

I started to cry, but my daddy laughed,
For he knew that I would find
When I turned around my marvelous toy
Came chuggin' from behind.

It went **ZIP** when it moved
And ***BOP*** when it stopped
And ***WHIRR*** when it stood still.
I never knew just what it was,
And I guess I never will.

Well, the years have gone by too quickly it seems.
I have my own little boy.
And yesterday I gave to him
My marvelous little toy.

His eyes nearly popped right out of his head.
He gave a squeal of glee.
Neither one of us knows just what it is,
But he loves it just like me.

It goes **ZIP** when it moves
And **BOP** when it stops
And **WHIRR** when it stands still.
I never knew just what it was,
And I guess I never will.

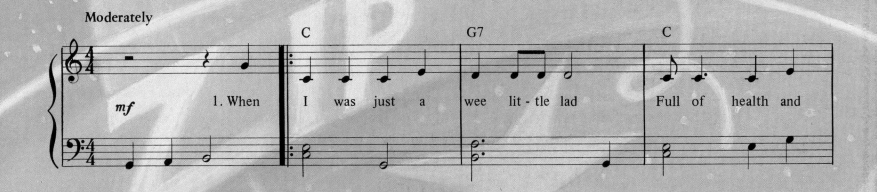

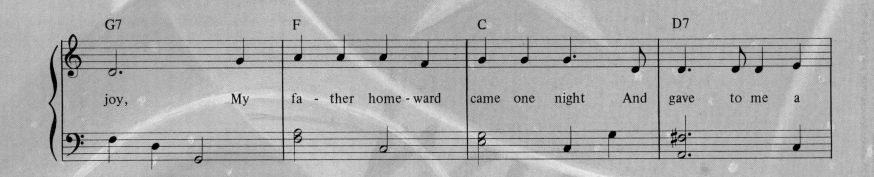